DREAMWORKS

# VOLTRON
### LEGENDARY DEFENDER

## Keith's Story WITHDRAWN

By Jesse Burton

Illustrated by Patrick Spaziante

Ready-to-Read

Simon Spotlight
New York   London   Toronto   Sydney   New Delhi

SIMON SPOTLIGHT
An imprint of Simon & Schuster Children's Publishing Division
1230 Avenue of the Americas, New York, New York 10020
This Simon Spotlight edition August 2018

For information about
special discounts for bulk purchases, please contact Simon & Schuster Special Sales at
1-866-506-1949 or business@simonandschuster.com.
Manufactured in the United States of America 0718 LAK
2 4 6 8 10 9 7 5 3 1
ISBN 978-1-5344-2041-0 (hc)
ISBN 978-1-5344-2040-3 (pbk)
ISBN 978-1-5344-2042-7 (eBook)

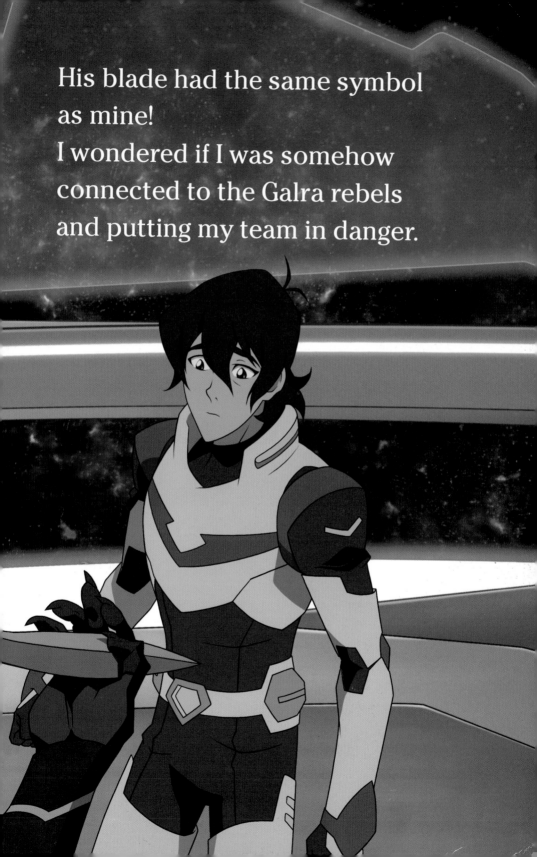

His blade had the same symbol as mine!
I wondered if I was somehow connected to the Galra rebels and putting my team in danger.

Shiro and I flew the Red Lion to the home base of the Blade of Marmora.

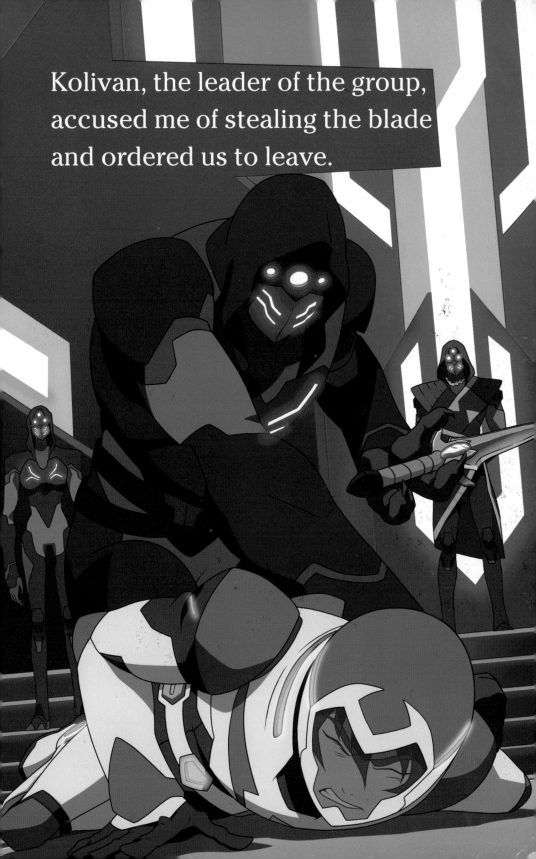

Kolivan, the leader of the group, accused me of stealing the blade and ordered us to leave.

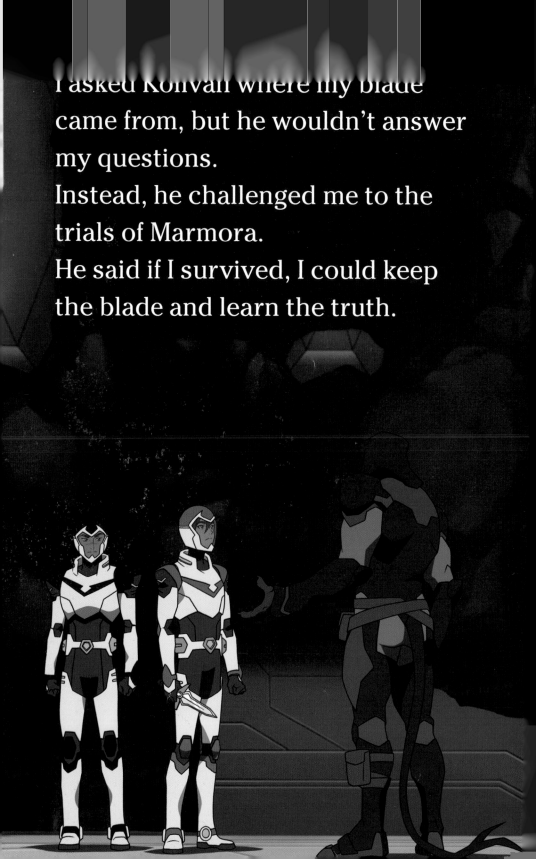

I asked Kolivan where my blade came from, but he wouldn't answer my questions.
Instead, he challenged me to the trials of Marmora.
He said if I survived, I could keep the blade and learn the truth.

In the first trial, I fought against just one fighter.
It wasn't easy, but I won!

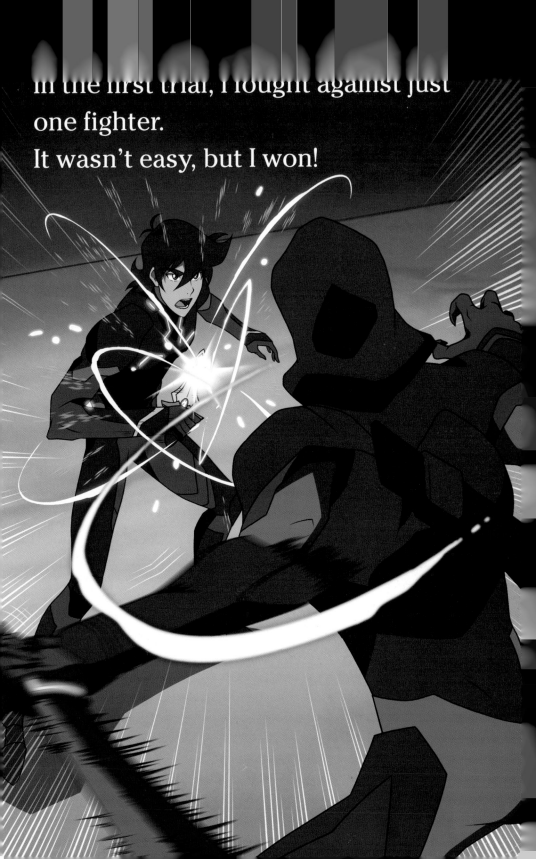

I ran through a doorway to a trial where I fought two fighters.
Each doorway led me to more and more fighters.
It seemed like it would never end.

Then I walked through a door that led me into a kind of dream.
My father was in the dream too.
He told me that my blade had belonged to my mother.
I wanted to know more, but then I woke up.

After all that, Kolivan still did not want to let me keep my blade. When I handed it over, something amazing happened.

The symbol on the blade glowed. "The only way this is possible is if you have Galra blood in your veins!" Kolivan said.

If what Kolivan said was true,
it meant I could be part alien!

I began to wonder if I belonged with the Blade of Marmora instead of with the Paladins.
It really made things confusing just when I was starting to feel like part of the team!

Then I realized that no matter where I came from, we were all on the same team.
I still don't have all the answers, but I hope to learn more as we work together to save the universe from Zarkon!

# KEITH

Keith was the most talented fighter pilot at the Galaxy Garrison, but flunked out. He refuses to live by other people's rules and instead carves out his own path. Keith is bonded to the Red Lion.

## STATS

- Member of the Blade of Marmora
- Birthday: October 23
- Heritage: part human, part Galra
- Age: 18

| | |
|---|---|
| STRENGTH | ///////////////////000000 |
| AGILITY | ///////////////////00000 |
| INTELLIGENCE | //////////////////000000 |

# RED LION
## Guardian Spirit of the Core

Voltron Position: right arm
Found: Galra battleship

## CAPABILITIES

- **Tail Laser:** moderately damages targets at long range
- **Mouth Cannon:** severely damages targets at long range
- **Jaw Blade:** cuts through targets at very close range
- **Magma Beam:** disintegrates target on contact
- **Hidden Power:** the Red Lion activates a plasma cannon

| | |
|---|---|
| DAMAGE | ///////////00000000000 |
| ARMOR | ////////////00000000000 |
| SPEED | ///////////////////00000 |

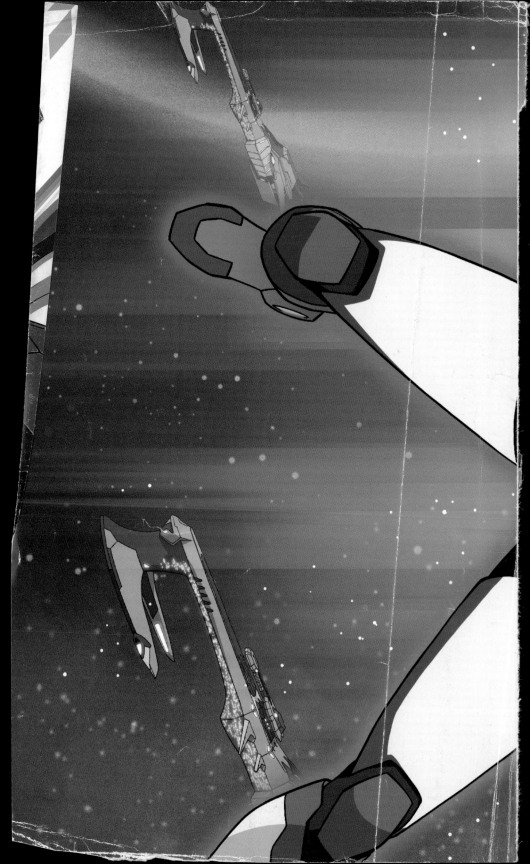

# COLLECT ALL SIX POSTERS TO FORM VOLTRON!

## FIND THE POSTERS IN THESE SIX PAPERBACK BOOKS:

*Allura's Story, Keith's Story, Lance's Story, Shiro's Story, Pidge's Story, Hunk's Story*